Charles Frederick Veil

Autobiography Of Charles F Veil

Charles Frederick Veil

Autobiography Of Charles F Veil

ISBN/EAN: 9783742854681

Manufactured in Europe, USA, Canada, Australia, Japa

Cover: Foto ©Andreas Hilbeck / pixelio.de

Manufactured and distributed by brebook publishing software
(www.brebook.com)

Charles Frederick Veil

Autobiography Of Charles F Veil

Autobiography

OF

Charles Frederick Veil

1813-1887

CHARLES FREDERICK VEIL

A Native German, Immigrant to America,
Tanner, Farmer, School Teacher, Merchant, Minister,
County Treasurer and Associate Judge in
Tioga County, Pennsylvania

"My times are in Thy Hands"—Psa. 31-15
Died Oct. 31,1887

AUTOBIOGRAPHY written by Charles Frederick Veil in his 67th year, A.D. 1879, commenced and continued from time to time. As I have arrived almost at the age allotted to man, by the Psalmist, and believing that a short history of my life might be of value and prove a source of satisfaction to my children and their descendents, I have concluded, yea feel it my duty, to write down the incidents of my life as they present themselves now after the lapse of so many years.

Parentage   I was born on the 11th day of February, A.D. 1813, in the town of Schorndorf, Kingdom of Wurtemberg in Germany. My father's name was Philip Heinrich Veil, my mother's name Fredrika nee Pfleiderer. They had seven children—Dorothy, the oldest, born August 1800 ; Carl Heinrich, born August 1802; Carl Gottlieb, born 1809; Caroline, born 1811; myself, Carl Frederick, 1813; Christian Frederick, born 1815, and Louisa born, 1819. My father, as also his father and grandfather, followed the trade of tanners, but at the same time owned sufficient land to raise their own bread, keep a small dairy and possessed a vineyard to supply their wants. While my parents could not be classed with the rich, they were sufficiently wealthy to be ranked with the best class of the burghers in the old town of Schorndorf, my birthplace. On account of their integrity and strictly moral character they enjoyed the general respect of their fellow citizens. My father, especially on account of his trade with many of the farmers in the adjoining villages, was not only very well-known but much loved and esteemed on account of his urbane manner, and strict integrity of dealing.

Schorndorf   A short description of my birthplace, the Oberamts stadt Schorndorf, as it now presents itself on memory's page, I deem in place here as towns similarly constructed and fortified are fast disappearing or have, as in the case of the town of my birth, been so much reconstructed, that they would be hardly recognized as the same towns at the present day. The old town, Schorndorf situated eighteen English miles or six Stunden East from Stuttgart the capital of Wurtemberg in the beautiful valley of the small river Rems, which connects with the

3

river Neckar at Neckar Rems, was a fortified town during the Thirty Years War and was after a siege by the Swedish army, then engaged in the defense of the Protestant faith, almost entirely destroyed, having but one memento of those trying times, which still remains. The part called the choir, probably so called from its use during the time before the Protestant religion was introduced in Wurtemberg, which choir is now a part of the only church in Schorndorf, and which still shows the more elaborate and decorated architecture of the Middle Ages.

The fortifications of the town remained the same up to the time when I had sufficient faculty of observation in my childhood. They consisted of a high inner wall with bastions, and in close connection with buildings of the town, outside of this wall and probably fifty rods wide all around the town was a flat terrain, mostly used for vegetable gardens. Next to this was a high embankment, called "Wall," which surrounded the town like a mountain range. At the foot of these embankments run a basin or ditch twenty feet deep and one hundred forty feet wide, which would be filled with water in time of a siege. Drawbridges placed at the only three outer gates, which give admission from East, North and West to the town, led to the entries of subterranean passageways or tunnels, walled and arched with the most solid masonry. These passages led underneath the above named embankments or ramparts, surrounding the town, to the iron inner gates and to the principal streets of the town itself.

"Redoubt Ramparts"

The streets of the town were built in a very irregular manner, being laid out more for the purpose of defense than beauty. Many buildings were placed out of the regular range, probably to afford shelter to the besieged, when the outer works had been taken by the enemy. A great part of these fortifications having become useless on account of the use of cannons and mortars in later years and the citizens being anxious to extend the limits of the town circumscribed by the Wall, embankments and ditches were torn down and leveled and converted into gardens or beautiful building lots. These improvements commenced in my childhood and have continued to the present time.

Bravery of Women

Schorndorf has been especially noted by the historians of Germany and German poets on heroic and brave conduct of its women during a siege by a French general in the Spanish Succession War. The legend tells of a council held by the burgomaster of Schorndorf and the principal burghers in which they had come to the conclusion to surrender the town to the French army. This result of the burghers deliberations in some way reached the ears of the burgomaster's wife, who immediately organized a band of women, equally disgusted with the cowardice of their lords and armed with brooms and whatever they could lay their hands on in the form of weapons. This formidable army of Amazons marched to the Court House where the men were in session and clamorously demanded a retraction of their resolution to surrender. The burghers, intimidated by their better halves gave in and being inspired by their wives with a better spirit, marched, led by the burgomaster's wife, to the walls, and made such a strong impression upon the French general that he raised the seige at once. This bold act of the women of Schorndorf was afterward sung by poets far and near who immortalized them, placing them with the wives of Weinsberg, who saved their husbands by strategy.

But, having been led astray by my love and affection for the old place, which gave me birth, it is high time that I should return to my life's history, as this is the principal object of these pages.

Early Childhood

Of my early childhood I have retained many vivid but painful recollections. At the age of four years I was afflicted with a disease of my eyes, which finally turned into cataracts, and a surgical operation became necessary to restore my eyesight. This operation was successfully performed by the King's chief surgeon, Dr. Kline, but in a very short time the disease returned and I had to submit to a second operation, which, although apparently successful as the first, also failed to give permanent relief, so that the surgeon despairing of the restoration of my eyesight by further operations, advised my parents to assist nature and time in my care by keeping a running sore on my arms to draw off the humors. This, after a lapse of about two years, produced a favorable effect upon my eyes. The films which covered the eyeballs became thinner and I well remember when I began to have indistinct glimpses of objects placed before my eyes. At the same time as the films were reduced the light striking my eyes caused great pains and I well remember how I crouched in the corner of the room to shut out the glare of light, so painful to my eyes. But by degrees I became more used to the light and as my eyes grew stronger my sight became more perfect and the light ceased to affect my eyes. While I am writing these lines in my sixty-seventh year without any spectacles my heart is filled with gratitude toward God for his mercies in restoring my sight, especially when I consider what my life would have been if I would have had to grope my way through the many years of my life without the great blessing of sight.

1822-27   When my eyesight was fully restored I had reached my eighth year and had therefore lost two years of the precious time of school instruction. My parents therefore at once sent me to school, but as I did not know my letters I became the butt of foolish jokes of the other boys of my age and was almost discouraged. But soon irritated by the sneers of my companions I came to the wise resolution to apply myself closely to my tasks and my efforts were so successful that after the expiration of one year of my school life and after a full examination I was promoted to the first place of the school of one hundred boys and had the honor to carry the banner of our school to the park arranged for the May Festival yearly held at that time in most all the schools in Germany. This success of the first year of my school life encouraged me to continue to progress through all the years of instruction before me with industry and close application to my studies. In my tenth year I was promoted to the lower department of the Latin School and after passing

6

through the intermediate department, I was placed in my twelfth year in the first department of the Latin schools. This department was taught by the principal of the Latin schools and Professors Schall and Caspar were noted as eminent teachers to such a degree that many boys from distant cities—Paris, Berlin, Stuttgart and other places—were placed under their instruction and care. About the same time I commenced the study of the French language and had sufficiently advanced to enable me to give private instruction in French to boys of my age for a small compensation, and I look back with pride to the time when I paid for the first dress coat which I ever wore by the earnings received from my pupils for tuition. When I arrived at the age of fourteen years, the limit of common school years, and after my confirmation in accordance with the established rules of the Lutheran church in which I was educated, the important question arose in the mind of my parents—what trade or profession should be chosen for me. As I had given indication of talent for drawing, we finally came to the conclusion

Vocation—
Architect

to choose the vocation of architect and I was placed as an apprentice to an architect in Stuttgart, Mr. Arnet, who was prominent on account of his proficiency in architectural drawings. While Mr. Arnet was perfectly well qualified to give instruction in drawing he was not equally well qualified to instruct in the practical part of architecture and not having many contracts for building, my chances for the practical study of architecture were not very good. I made good progress in drawing but did not do so well in the cutting of stones, which part of practice I was to learn. After remaining in Stuttgart three

1827-30

years the old disease of my eyes began to make its appearance, my eyes became irritated and by the advice of surgeons I had to leave the chosen field of life and return home where I had to remain confined to the house on account of the weakness of my eyes which could not bear the light and being persuaded that no business in life, which would require a close application of the eyes could be followed by me without danger of losing my eyesight entirely. I was obliged to choose a trade suitable, and as

7

my father was then without assistance my two older brothers, Henry and Gottlieb being then in Italy where Henry had established a tannery, I went into the tannery, which being a shop dimly lighted, was then the most congenial to my weak eyes.

Being again under my parents' roof it may be well to take a retrospective look into the history of our family up to the time I had arrived at the age of 17 years.

My oldest sister, Dorothy, had been married ten years 1821 before to Ludwig Kraiss, a young saddler, who established himself in business in Schorndorf. My brother, Henry, after having traveled extensively in Germany, Hungary, Italy and France, had returned home while I was on a visit at Schorndorf during my apprenticeship at Stuttgart. His arrival at home was entirely unexpected, which was by him improved by representing himself as a friend intimately acquainted with our brother Henry. He failed to disguise his feelings long, but made himself known as Henry but so much changed was he that no one in the family would recognize him as such. Our mother, who might have been expected by a mother's instinct to have recognized him, the first, was the most obstinate in refusing to recognize and acknowledge him as her son. It was therefore only after the most positive proofs of his identity that he was recognized and welcomed as a son and brother. This farcical incident is still fresh in my memory, and often did we laugh over the scenes presented that evening in our family circle.

Brother Henry remained only about three months at home and, fascinated with the beauty of Italian skies, he again left his home and finally erected in partnership with a cousin-a merchant at Leghorn, a tannery in the Granduchy of Tuscany at Barco, a small town 18 miles west from Florence. My second brother, Gottlieb, soon after Henry's departure to Italy left home on his travels, as it was then the rule or law in Germany that every young man, after having served his apprenticeship had to travel three years before he could set up in trade as master. Before I had commenced to work in the tannery my brother Gottlieb returned to subject himself to conscription, and after having been freed from military duty left home again to join his brother Henry in Italy. My sisters, Caroline and Louisa, remained at their home, while my youngest brother, Christian, was a merchant's clerk in Stuttgart. Such was the position of our family while I was at home learning the trade of a tanner. After

Journeyman

serving an apprenticeship of only 18 months I was promoted as a journeyman and as my brother, Gottlieb, had again returned from Italy I was free in my 19th year to commence my travels.

1832 Travels

Before the commencement of my travels I worked three months as journeyman in Goppingen, which was recommended by my prudent father, as a trial or test of my capacity to fill the position of a journeyman. Full of eager anticipations of the pleasure to travel from place to place and to see cities and countries new to me I left home in April 1832 with many admonitions from my parents accompanied with their blessings and best wishes of success. It may be proper to say here that all these travels of journeymen were made on foot and under strict and sometimes severe police rules and restrictions. Everyone desiring to travel had to provide himself with a passport in the shape of a blank book containing about 100 pages in the front of which a full description and signature of the person or bearer is given. At each prominent police station this passport had to be presented and examined by the director of the police who entered his visa to proceed to the indicated important police station on the route the traveler wished to take. All these visas or permits had to be sealed with the coat of arms or wappen of the town or city where the permit was

Ulm

given. I left the kingdom of Wurtemberg at Ulm—at the river Danube—a great fortress. When I arrived at the opposite side of the Danube I had to submit to an examination of my passport by the Bavarian guard and upon presentation or production of $10 in money, as a proof that I had sufficient means to pass through the kingdom of Bavaria, I was permitted to pass beyond the frontier of Wurtemberg into Bavaria.

Bavaria is in general, as far as I traversed it on my

9

travels, a very fertile country—the inhabitants of very robust physique and much given to pleasure seeking. The general prevailing religion of the people is Roman Catholic, although there are large districts, especially in Franconia or Pfalz, where the Protestant religion prevails. The first city of importance on my tour was the ancient city of Augsburg, where the Protestant princes and divines met the Emperor Charles V during the Reformation, and entered their protest against the false doctrines of the Roman church, and published their confession of faith in public council. From Augsburg I went by Auspach to the antiquated city of Nurnberg, formerly a free and independent city. The city is built in a very quaint way—houses on principal streets mostly four stories high, each story projecting about five or six feet over the one below it, which gives the streets almost the appearance of arches. From Nurnberg I traveled by Erlangen, a German University, and very neatly and regularly built, (the old town having been destroyed by fire) to Bamberg on the river Main and from there to Saxe Coburg, capital of one of the many Saxon dukedoms and principalities. Prince Albert, husband of Queen Victoria, was born in this small city and while on a visit at St. James Court was so fortunate to gain the affection of the young Queen of England. From Coburg I passed through Meiningen, Hildburghausen, Schwazburg Sondershousen, Saxe Gotha, Weimar, Altenburg, all small Saxon dukedoms and reached Leipsic, the great city of fairs and now noted for the many publishing houses there established.

Leipsic is a very old city and made famous on account of the great battle fought here in October 1813, when the power of Napoleon Bonaparte received the first great shock, and the German powers by union showed their strength. From Leipsic I went by Halle, another German University, to Magdeburg in Prussia (Brandenburg) also an old city and noted in the history of the Thirty Year War, as having suffered terribly during a seige. After leaving Magdeburg I passed through Braunschweig to Hannover, a very fine city with parks. I had now traveled constantly for twelve weeks without finding work

Augsburg

Nurnberg

1832

Leipsic

10

in any of the tanneries, at which I had called for the purpose of obtaining work. Business of every kind seemed
to be prostrated on account of the prevalence of cholera
in the cities of northern Germany. At Hannover I heard
of a tanner in an adjoining town who was then in need of
the services of a tanner, or rather currier, to finish leather
for the Brunswick fair. Upon application I was engaged
and was very glad to rest a while from my weary travels,
which at the time had lost much of their former attrac-
tions and anticipated pleasures. I found the people very
kind but had much difficulty to understand their dialect,
as they spoke plattdeutsch or low dutch. After remaining
about four weeks, during which time we finished all the
tanned leather on hand to be exposed to sale at
Brunswick fair, which commenced soon afterwards, I
left again on my way to Bremen, a German seaport.
From Bremen I went in company with an elderly
Hamburger who was on his return from extensive
travels in North and South America, and who enter-
tained me very much with vivid descriptions of the
countries which he had seen during his travels. I have
no doubt that he did not always adhere to the truth,
but kept drawing very heavily upon his large stores of
imagination.

The country between Bremen and Hamburg is very
level, generally poor soil and large herds of cattle are
roving in the meager pastures. After many laughable incidents on our journey we arrived at Hamburg, the
principal seaport of Germany, and like Bremen and
Lubeck, a free Hause Stadt, or commercial city. Hamburg has very narrow streets, which on account of the
height of the buildings (mostly five or six stories
high) seem like mere alleys crowded to the utmost by
vehicles of every kind and pedestrians along the narrow side walks. It was here at Hamburg where cholera, at the time I was there, raged most fearfully. After having seen persons falling on the sidewalks
struck down suddenly by this terrible disease I
deemed it unsafe to remain longer, but after having
my passport examined I made good to Berlin.

11

I left in Company with two Hessian journeymen tanners on Our way to Lauenburg and Berlin. After traveling along the sandy road 15 or 16 miles We were very much tired and tried to obtain a night's rest in one of the small hamlets, but when the people heard that we came from Hamburg they refused to take us in for fear of being infected with cholera. After several rejected applications we adopted the strategy to pass around the next village and, apparently coming from the opposite direction, we were finally admitted to a hostelry. After a very frugal supper were led by the landlord, in company with several traveling Jews, to the barn where we were ordered to mount a wagon loaded with barley to quarter there during the night. The landlord prepared a bed of straw for the traveling Jews along side of the wagon and left us to enjoy our rest, the best we could. Although very much tired myself and one of the Hessians could not sleep on account of being continually pricked and tickled by the bristle ears of barley while our comrade, who was of a more phlegmatic disposition soon commenced to snore. This made us more nervous and my waking comrade suggested that I should give a push the sleeper to stop his snoring which I did very promptly, but alas, our poor comrade lost his equilibrium and with his knapsack, on which he rested, tumbled from the wagon and landed, knapsack and all, amongst the Jews who, being suddenly a wakened, as by an earthquake, commenced to howl in their fear. During the confusion our poor comrade, fully a wakened by his fall, de his way back to the barley wagon and when the landlord awakened by the loud outcries of the Jews, arrived with a lantern to ascertain the cause of this great commotion, we commenced a concert of snoring declaring thereby our entire innocence of the disturbance. The Jews, not being able to give a satisfactory reason for their disturbance, were severely reprimanded by the landlord with the intimation that he should drive them from barn if they should again disturb his rest during the night. The Jews removed their bed of straw to the side of the barn and after full quiet was restored I finally ob-

12

tained some sleep. I had not slept long when I discovered that there was some animal at our wagon and plainly heard the munching of the barley. I was very much provoked at this new disturbance and on the impulse of the moment gave a kick in the direction where I heard the noise and found it to be a horse who had got loose in his stall and was attracted to the barley wagon. The horse sprung suddenly back and, in trying to reach his stall in his sudden retreat, trampled upon the Jews and created a perfect pandemonium amongst them. The landlord again appeared upon the scene of action, armed with a formidable cart whip. We on the barley wagon again resumed our snoring concert to prove our innocence and the poor Jews were not withstanding all their remonstrances driven by the landlord from the barn, while we three innocents removed our quarters from the elevated position on the barley wagon to the more humble straw bed of the Jews from which they were so ruthlessly driven by the infuriated landlord. This laughable incident has always remained fresh in my memory and I have here related it, to give an instance of the many ludicrous experiences of my journeyings. In connection with this and to give a proper idea of the construction of the farm houses in the northern part of Germany, I will add here a description of the same.

North German Farm Houses

The farm buildings resemble our barns in their outer appearances. As you enter in the front gable end you have before you a long threshing floor and to the right and left are ranged the stalls of horses and cattle. At the end of the threshing floor without, any partition whatever, is erected a large hearth with a tunnel-shaped cover to take in the smoke escaping through chimney. On this hearth all the cooking for the family is done. In the rear of this kitchen runs a partition across the building with a door to the living rooms of the family. With the exception of the larger towns, travelers are generally accommodated with straw, spread on the floor, instead of beds, which proves very inconvenient to travelers accustomed to good beds which are universally found in the southern part of Germany. My first experience of

13

sleeping on straw in Saxony was far from agreeable, but I finally got so accustomed to it that I could sleep as soundly on the coarse straw, having my knapsack or the back of a chair for my head to rest on, as I ever slept on a good feather bed.

After traveling by a short day's journey through northeastern Prussia we arrived at Berlin, the capital of Prussia, where we remained about a week to see all the prominent buildings and museums in this city noted for its beauty and splendid buildings. From Berlin I went to Potsdam, saw the palace of Sans Souci, the favorite palace and residence of Frederick the Great. At Potsdam I heard the first musical bell chime on one of the steeples. The bells playa tune every hour. I had also the satisfaction of seeing a grand review of the Prussian army, which was very fine in appearance. The King, himself, was present and had at this review the misfortune to be thrown from his horse.

Wittenberg From Potsdam I traveled south to Wittenberg, saw the old church at the gates of which Martin Luther posted his thesis of protests against Roman (papal) indulgences at the beginning of the Reformation. On the public place near the same church is erected the bronze monument with the statue of Dr. Luther.

From Wittenberg I went to Halle—another German university and noted by the orphan school instituted by the great philanthropist August Franke and by Naumburg through the small Saxon principalities to Coburg on the Bavarian frontiers. Here I found myself checked by a cordon or guard of soldiers, who were posted on the northern boundaries of Bavaria, to maintain a quarantine on account of the cholera prevailing with more or less violence in the north of Germany. The time fixed for quarantine by the government of Bavaria was two weeks. This impediment on my journey was connected with much hardships, as I was entirely destitute of money to pay for my board during the two weeks and being obliged to remain under the surveillance of the guard. I would not rely upon the support of master tanners who have an organization and treasury from which

14

the traveling journeymen are supported. I will always remember with gratitude the benevolence and liberality of the peasantry along the frontier, who by free gifts of provisions relieved the wants of all those who had no means, like myself. At the close of the quarantine imposed I was permitted to leave and entering Bavaria again much humbled in spirit and considerably wiser than when I entered at Ulm and full of glorious anticipations of the pleasures of travel I reached Bamberg, where my passport had to be revised and where I ought to have again shown and produced $10 to the police which I had not—the last penny having long before left my purse. The director of the police after examination of my passport, when he found that I had not been in employment for many weeks, and that I was entirely stripped of money entered on the passport the direction to travel by the nearest route to the frontiers of Wurtemberg and home. This entry grieved me very much as I was very unwilling to return home so soon but I had to follow directions and with a heavy heart I took the road to Wurzburg, another old Franconian city, and from there toward the nearest town in Wurtemberg, Mergentheim.

At Bishofsheim, in Baden, but 15 miles distant from the frontiers of Baden and Wurtemberg I arrived late one evening, very tired and very hungry, having traveled the whole day without tasting any food whatever. There being but two small tanneries in the town, I received but a very small allowance from the treasury, very little more than what I wanted to pay for lodging overnight, and the little food, which I was able to buy, but stimulated my hunger the more. That evening was the most sorrowful time I ever experienced in my life, and my forsaken situation depressed me to such a degree that I could not restrain bitter tears. While I was sitting alone in a corner of the inn where I intended to lodge, but as the proverb says "the night is darkest just before day," so all the darkness which had oppressed me, was suddenly dispersed. Just as I was about retiring to rest, hungry and distressed in mind, a gentleman, who during

15

the evening was playing billiards with others came into the room from the adjoining billiard room, and inquired for the traveling journeyman tanner. I arose timidly, not knowing the character of the gentleman and being afraid that he might be a police officer, and replied that I was the person inquired for. After several questions relative my home and the places where I had last been employed, he asked the welcome question whether I desired to obtain employment. I gladly responded that it would be my greatest wish to be so fortunate to find work, when he told me that I might commence work next morning at his tannery in the town. Before I retired to rest, with my heart full of joy and gratitude toward God, who sent this timely deliverance in my time of utmost need, I could not help but offer my heartfelt thanks to God. After a good night's rest I commenced to work and found my employer and family, although Roman Catholic, very kind. Having traveled so long I had become destitute of clothes and shoes and, therefore, felt myself obliged to write my parents for assistance in money to provide myself again with decent clothing, etc.. which request was cheerfully complied with.

After remaining at Bishofsheim about four months during which time I was fully recruited in strength and I was so imprudent to listen to the overtures of a fellow workman who wished to leave the place on a journey to see distant countries and cities. He offered to assist me in meeting the expenses of a long journey to Vienna. As I always had a great desire to see as much of the world as I possibly could during the term of my travels, I finally yielded and in company with my colleague and in opposition to the remonstrances of my kind employer, left Bishofsheim and we traveled toward Frankfort on the Main. We had only progressed two or three days on our journey when my colleague's courage and desire to travel abated to such a degree that he anxiously inquired for work, offering his services for half price. If I had not been ashamed, I would have returned to Bishofsheim, as I had a standing offer of my employer, that he would give me employment whenever I would return. But false

16

pride prevented me, and on the morning following the day, when my colleague cowardly had forsaken me, I went to the police officer where both our passports had been deposited. These passports or books are generally placed in pasteboard cases and when I asked for my passport the police officer handed both passports deposited in the evening and I carelessly reached for my well-known case as mine, while by the carelessness of the officer the cases had been changed. Without any misgivings on my part, and believing all was right, I proceeded on my journey toward Frankfurt. At Ashaffenberg I took passage in a market boat to Frankfurt, where I arrived, without any interference from any Gendarm or police officer. Immediately on my arrival at the inn where tanners have their home (for in every town in Germany the homes of the traveling journeymen of the several trades are respectively assigned and distributed to the several hotels in each town) I was told by the landlord (called Herbergs Vater) that there was work for a tanner in the city. I was very glad to hear the good news, as it was then in the middle of winter when the prospect of obtaining work in tanneries was riot very bright.

Upon application I found work, but was directed to deposit my passport at the p6lice directory, and when I arrived at the office I found that I had my colleague's passport in my case and I shall never forget the consternation which I felt upon this discovery. With faltering voice I told to the clerks present the position in which I found myself, but instead of sympathy these quill drivers loaded me with execrations and exulted in the idea of having trapped a great villian. Conscious of my innocence, I resented their revilings which caused considerable commotion and uproar when they rang the bell for the jailor to put me in prison. But during the noise of the altercation a side door opened and the director of police appeared upon the scene and inquired for the cause of the disturbance. Both clerks vociferously informed their superior that they had caught a villian, which accusation I energetically denied. The director, who was a fine appearing gentleman, then commanded silence and re-

17

quested me to state the difficulty, which I did in a humble manner. After courteously listening to my explanation and severely reprimanding his clerks on account of their violent manner, he told them the great truth—that every person should be treated as innocent until he was proven guilty. He then requested me to follow him into his private office, where he took my deposition and told me, that he would forward the protocol prepared with the exchanged passport to Mittenberg where the exchange of passports was made and if I had stated the truth my passport would be forwarded and all things would be made right.

Under the circumstances I could not enter upon work but should remain under the surveillance of the police until suspicion would be removed by the exchange of passports. He gave me a permit to remain at Frankfurt and directed me to show myself every morning at the police station. After the expiration of five days, when my passport was still unexchanged by the Mittenberg authorities, suspicion was raised even in the mind of the director, who had shown so much kindness before, and my permit was curtailed by the injunction to present myself hourly at the station which was almost equivalent to imprisonment. But at the expiration of the second day, after this severe restriction, my passport was received by the director and everything substantiated as I had stated in my deposition. The director regretted that I had lost the employment (which in the meantime had been given to another traveling tanner) and gave the good advice to be more careful in the future. I have narrated this incident to show how strictly the police watch over the multitudes of tramping journeymen.

Description of Frankfurt

While I was retained in Frankfurt I had a very good opportunity to view the city, which is quite old but celebrated on account of the large fairs held there, at which merchants of many nations yearly meet for exchange of their different wares and commodities. At these fairs there is a large business done at wholesale, orders for goods taken and received. In one of the oldest streets of Frankfurt I saw the quaint old residence of the oldest member of the Rothschild's. The finest street in Frankfurt is the Quay, along the river Main, which is spanned by a beautiful stone bridge connecting Frankfurt with Sachsenhausen, a suburb of the city. The German diet used to assemble at Frankfurt, being one of the free cities of Germany, and in ancient times the German Emperors were crowned there.

While I awaited the return of my passport the landlord of the hotel where I stayed received a notice that a tanner was wanted at Koenigstein, in the dukedom of Nassau, 15 miles from Frankfurt, and immediately after matters were righted I went to Koenigstein where I found employment, remaining until spring had fully opened, when the travel fever attacked me again. I went from Koenigstein to Wiesbaden, the capital of Nassau and a great watering place, from there to Koblenz on the Rhine, Bingen and Mainz at the mouth of the river Main. Mainz was a confederate fortress, occupied by troops of Prussia, Austria and Hesse, Damstadt, who jointly guarded the fortifications. I passed here over the long boat bridges across the Rhine.

From Mainz I traveled by Worms, where Dr. Martin Luther, the great Reformer, appeared in the defense of his doctrine before the papal Cardinal and princes of Germany, to Manheim, a very fine and modern city with wide regular streets.

From Manheim I passed through Heidelberg, the great German university, where every traveler is anxious to see the world renowned wine cask in the castle cellar, to Heilbron on the river Nekar and by Pforzheilh, the city of Goldsmith near the Black Forest to Gernsbach in the valley of the Murg. Remaining there over Sabbath I met accidentally a master tanner, who, upon learning my home and name insisted that I should work for him, for the only reason because about 40 years before he had worked for my father in Schorndorf. To accommodate him and to satisfy his singular whim I remained with him about two months after which time I followed on my route through Baden-Baden, another great watering resort and along the foot of the Black Forest range of

19

mountains to Shafhausen, a Swiss town on the Rhine and near its falls.

From Shaffhausen I went with my cousin Louis Veil, whom I accidentally met in Shaffhausen to Zurich, the home of the great Swiss Reformer Ulric Zwingle, and along the beautiful lake of Zurich, through the romantic mountain scenery of the Upper Cantons of Switzerland to Chur in Graubundten, surrounded by snow covered mountains. Here I again went into a tannery to work entirely upon the reputation of my name. The owner of the tannery, Mr. Price, told me that my oldest brother, Henry, had worked for him several years ago, and he was so well pleased with him, that he wanted me, his brother, to work for him. As the master tanner was noted as a first class finisher of leather and I, therefore, believed that I could learn much while in his employ, I consented and worked in his currying shop about three months, but on account of his violent temper which sometimes broke out in such sudden bursts that it was truly unsafe to be about him, I again left and passing through Tyrol I reached Lindau, a Bavarian town on the shore of Lake Constance, where I again worked for two months.

From there I returned to Ulm, the city where I had first crossed the frontiers of Wurtemberg into Bavaria, and there again to work in a large tannery, where I remained until the time when I had to return home to be subjected to Conscription.

On my arrival home I was gladly welcomed by parents, brother Gottlieb, and sisters. My younger brother, Christian, was then in Rheims, bookkeeper of a large mercantile house and my oldest brother still remained in Italy, but had failed in business, and was then preparing to emigrate to America. This intention of my brother, connected with the many trials which I had just undergone in my travels, and the general stagnation of business in Germany raised the wish in my mind to join my brother Henry in America.

My parents would have opposed any such plan if their anxiety for the welfare of Henry, who had been unfortunate before, had not turned the balance and prompted them to yeild to my wishes. In the Conscription I was so fortunate to draw the number next to the highest, which cleared me from military duty, but honesty prompts me to acknowledge that I would have been rejected on account of size—being 1/10 inch too short. As soon as I was free from the Conscription I made my preparation to go to America without any intention of remaining there permanently.

I and a young friend, Otto Klemm, whose widowed mother was anxious that he should accompany me to join his brother in America, made a contract wit at Stuttgart for our passage from Havre de Grae, a French seaport, to New York and here I would add my advice founded upon my own experience to all emigrants, that it is at all times the best to postpone making contracts for passage, until they arrive at the port where they intend to embark. We would have made a much more favorable contract at Havre and could have had passage in a superior ship if we had not previously contracted and had, therefore, to abide by the contract made at Stuttgart.

On the 15th day of April, 1834, after having bid farewell to brothers, sisters, parents, and other near relatives, I left home accompanied by my brother, Gottlieb as far as Stuttgart. We went on foot through Pforzheim, Baden-Baden to Strasburg, where we took the Diligence (stage coach) to Paris and arrived there after three days, passing through beautiful and fertile France. We remained at Paris a whole week to see all the curiosities of this splendid city. After having inspected the great

monuments of art, architecture and Parisian life, we took passage on a small steam boat to Havre, but found the passage very tedious, the river Seine being very low.

We passed through the ancient city Rouen, whose Cathedral is noted not only for antiquity but also on account of the quaint Gothic architecture. On the square near the Cathedral is the monument of Joan of Arc, who was burned by the English, condemned as a witch. Rouen we passed more expediously down the river and

21

after being four days on our journey from Paris arrived at Havre, one of the best havens or ports of the Eastern world. Immediately on our arrival, myself and companion went to the mercantile house, which was in connection with the house in Stuttgart, which had made the contract with us. We found that a brig was then ready to sail within a week, and a berth was assigned to us in the same. Upon inquiry on board the brig we found it already so full and the accommodations so poor, that we came to the conclusion we'd rather wait for the next vessel than to be crowded in the brig. If we had not already paid for our passage we might have sailed in one of the regular American packets for less fare and with much better accommodations.

After waiting ten days we embarked in a French ship, Fort Royal, with 250 emigrants—German, Swiss and French, and on the 10th day of May, 1834, we sailed out of the harbor, and soon lost sight of land, and very soon that terrible disease, seasickness, had hold of me and I was suffering from its effects for two long weeks, during which time I was almost tired of life and often wished that I had remained on terra firma. When I was finally free from seasickness and my appetite returned, prospects commenced to brighten and while I had viewed everything around me with gloomy eyes, I now began to take a more cheering view of everything. My acquaintance with the French language was now very useful, as many difficulties between German and French emigrants took place on account of not understanding each other, and the captain, who only spoke French, had to use me as an interpreter between contending parties, which prompted him to extend many courtesies to me. I was often invited in the cabin and was continually posted, relative to progress of the ship. Before we were many days at sea, we found that our ship was a very slow sailer. Many of the American ships more snugly built passed us. Near the Azore Islands we were becalmed for almost two weeks, where we had the volcano Teuinffe constantly before our eyes.

After leaving the Azores we had more tempestuous

weather, and amongst many others encountered a storm lasting three days, during which time the hatches were closed and the steerage passengers kept below; almost suffocated in the foul air. By the kindness of the captain I was permitted to remain on deck and in his cabin during most all the storms, and thereby escaped the sufferings of the passengers confined in the steerage. After having been on the sea for 50 days, we finally heard the welcome sound "land!" and soon afterwards a pilot boat came alongside and the pilot took command of our vessel and we entered the New York Bay. To our right and to our left we had the most pleasing view of the American shores, which appeared to us, after our long sea voyage, like an enchanted landscape.

We soon arrived at the Quarantine, where a general cleaning, washing and fumigation took place in preparation of the medical examination, which was to take place the next day.

On the following morning all the emigrants dressed in their best clothes, were mustered on deck, examined by the Quarantine physician. All trunks, chests, etc., belonging to the passengers were examined by the Customhouse officers and contraband goods confiscated without mercy. Soon after this ordeal of medical and legal examination a towboat came along side of the Quarantine New York, grounds in which we embarked for the city of New York. 1834 We landed on the North River and found the landing full of friends of emigrants and runners of boarding houses. Myself and companion went with one of the latter gentry to the boarding house with the sign of William Tell in Greenwich Street, and where we obtained a room on the second floor of the hotel—fifty-three days after our embarkation at Havre.

Before we left the Quarantine grounds we heard the booming of cannons in the direction of the city of New York which continued and became louder as we approached the city in the tug-boat. As We were not vain enough to believe that the salutes were in honor of our arrival, we could not account for the demonstrations, which increased as we landed and passed up the street.

23

On every hand we found the American flag displayed and young America busy in firing firecrackers, many of them exploded in the midst of female squads of emigrants to their utter consternation, and our first impression of American character was certainly not very flattering. As we proceeded through all this tumult to our boarding house, which was fortunately not very distant from the wharf where we had landed, the apparent mystery was solved when the landlord, being questioned, informed us, that this being the 4th day of July, they were celebrating the anniversary of American independence. During the afternoon we strolled to the Battery where we were regaled with a review of New York military troops and had the first glimpse of the free and easy manner and discipline of American soldiery .

The first impression made was far from favorable as we were accustomed to the fine drills of European standing armies. After remaining a few days at New York, which city, then in the year 1834, was far inferior in appearance to the present New York, or other European cities which I had visited during my travels.

My companion, Otto Klemm separated from me and left by steamer to Albany and from there west to Ohio, where his brother then resided. I went by steamer to New Brunswick and by the first railroad of America, and first I ever saw and traveled on, to Trenton on the Dela-
ware, where we again took a steamer to Philadelphia, the Quaker city, where I found lodgings in Fifth Street, then almost the western boundary of the city. I was very favorably impressed with the general appearance of the city, and found it upon closer inspection superior to any other city which I had seen, especially in regard to cleanliness and regularity of the streets which are wide and run parallel and in rectangles from north to south and east to west. The streets running north and south, except Front Street along the Delaware River, are numbered and the streets running from the river west are mostly named by the shade trees planted along the same, such as Chestnut, Walnut, Cherry, Spruce, Almond, Poplar, etc. The only exception to the city was the unifor-

mity of its brick buildings, with marble steps and cope I stones which are always kept clean and white. This uniformity has at this time been much remedied by the erection of many splendid buildings, public and private, with marble fronts, which give the city such a pleasing appearance that it is now universally admitted to be one, of the most beautiful cities in the world.

After remaining in the city sufficient time to see its most prominent buildings and parks, I traveled on foot, leaving my effects at my boarding house, through Philadelphia and Montgomery Counties to Sancond near Allentown, at which place lived Jacob Heyler, a tanner, the son of my master in Goeppingen, who had given me a letter of recommendation to his son. Here I expected to hear news of my brother, Henry, who intended to sail from Italy to America and whom I had requested to apply either personally or by letter to Mr. Heyler so that we would be able to find each other in America. Upon inquiry I found that Henry had not as yet been heard from and I returned to Philadelphia, but on my way I obtained work in Quakertown with a Quaker, the bargain having been made by an interpreter, as I did not understand any English and the Quaker no German. When I commenced work in the tannery I found to my consternation that there were two colored tanners working in the same and having previously hardly ever seen a negro, except on exhibition, my prejudice prompted me to leave again as fast as I could. This foolish act on my part, whenever I think of it, causes me to smile at my own folly.

The same day when I left Quakertown I found work in a tannery at Doylestown, Bucks County, with Thomas Wambold, a Pennsylvania German. As business and times were not very brisk at that time in the United States on account of the action of President A. Jackson against the United States bank, I was fortunate to obtain work so soon, although at the low wages of $6 per month. I remained at Doylestown from the latter part of July until Christmas without hearing any news of the whereabouts of my brother Henry and I had almost de-

25

spaired to learn his fate, when I received a letter of him from Milford, Pike County, in which I received the information that my brother had landed in New York in August and was now employed in a tannery at Milford and that he had obtained my address from Mr. Heyler, and that he desired very much that I should come to him, especially as I could obtain work in the immediate neighborhood at much better wages than I was then receiving.

When I informed my employer of my intention to leave he insisted that I should remain with him, offering me the same wages and the free loan of horse and wagon to convey me on a visit to my brother I was finally persuaded to accept the offer, but felt timid to drive a horse that distance, as I had never driven a horse before in my life. Mr. Wambold went with me to teach me the handling of the ribbons and guidance of the horse, three miles on my journey, when I ventured alone and after several blunders on my part and damage to the wagon I arrived safely at Milford where I found my brother Henry whom I had not seen for seven years. He did not recognize me at first and was very glad to see me when I made myself known. After having a very agreeable visit with him I returned to Doylestown, where I remained until the 15th day of April, 1835, being just one year from the time when I left my home.

I had received letters of Otto Klemm, my companion on the voyage across the Atlantic, in which he gave glowing descriptions of the West, which prompted me to leave the East. I traveled by stage to Philadelphia, and from there by steamboat and railroad to New York. From New York I went by steamboat to Albany on the Hudson River where I made a contract for my conveyance and board on a canal boat to Buffalo, Which journey consumed eleven days now made by rail in about 12 hours. What a contrast in the mode and expedition in traveling.

When I arrived at Buffalo, at that time but a small town, I found that my further progress West on Lake Erie was checked, the harbor of Buffalo being blockaded with masses of ice. This was on the 1st day of May, 1835, *(Age 22)* when the spring was very late. As there was no prospect

26

of my further progress for a few days at least I took occasion to visit my cousin, William Veil, who was stationed at North Boston, twenty miles from Buffalo, as pastor of a Lutheran congregation. As I was not very favorably impressed with the surroundings and the position of my cousin I did not extend my visit, but returned on the third day to Buffalo, whose port was still locked with ice. On the 10th day of May I learned that a steamer would leave Black Rock, three miles below Buffalo, for Detroit. I had my trunk taken down and took passage on board the steamer, Michigan, on the evening before our departure in the early morning. During the night a south wind drove the masses of ice out of the Buffalo harbor which came floating down the Niagara River and threatened the destruction of our boat at Black Rock. The captain of our boat, an impetuous and very profane man, swore that our boat should be the first in Detroit, and steam being up, we pushed through the driving masses of ice, continually breaking against the side of the vessel, toward the Canada shore which was more free of the floating ice. While I was standing on the forepart of the steamer I felt a trembling under my feet connected with a rumbling noise and immediately after, we were fast on a rock and unable to proceed an inch forward or backward. At the same time, looking over toward Buffalo, we saw steamers leaving on their way to the West. The captain of the boat, highly incensed at our misfortune, which by proper sounding, might easily have been avoided, sent a boat across to Buffalo to solicit the aid of two tug boats to move us from our position on the rocks, and very soon they came near us, one of the same by some mismanagement staving, with its bowsprit, a big hole on our boat's side. While the other tried to pull us by cable chains from the rock on which we had stranded. But all proved vain, as we were so firmly fixed on the rock that only the lighting of our boat could bring relief. All the male passengers were therefore ordered to get on board of one of the tug boats which had been placed on the side of our steamer. As soon as the greater part of the male passengers had placed themselves on board

27

of the tug our steamer rose from the rock and commenced to move. We scrambled over the sides, back to our boat, and being entirely free from the rocks, continued our voyage. When all difficulties were removed some of the boats, which had left Buffalo harbor in the morning, were a considerable distance on their way, and our captain ordered the steam to be raised to such a degree that we might redeem lost time. But all the captain's foolhardy efforts proved vain, as the engines were impaired, and could not work well, and after a whole day's fruitless efforts to repair the damage, we had to land at Fairview and have our machinery repaired at a machine shop.

Cleveland

When we arrived on the third day at Cleveland, I was glad to leave the boat and instead of proceeding to Detroit I took the Ohio Canal and went from Cleveland to Massilon, and from there by stage to Wooster , Wayne County, Ohio, where my companion, Otto Klemm, and his brother, Adolph, were employed as clerks in a large store, fifteen miles from Wooster. At Mount Eaton I found work and in the immediate neighborhood I found many of my French and Swiss fellow passengers on the Fort Royal, who had settled down as farmers and mechanics. After remaining at Mt. Eaton about three months and having made the experience that money was much scarcer in the West than in the East, so that I had to take all my wages, $12 per month, in store trade, I left with intention to return to Pennsylvania.

I went by boat to Zanesville on Muskingum River and by stage on the National Road to Wheeling, W. Va., where I took passage on an Ohio steam boat to Pittsburgh. Pittsburgh was then in its infancy of its manufacturing greatness, and was not very attractive in its appearance.

Johnstown

From Pittsburgh I traveled by canal to Johnstown, Cambria, County, at the foot of the range of the Allegheny Mountains. Here I again found work and while there I received a letter from my brother, Henry, which was forwarded to me from Doylestown, by a friend with whom I had kept up a correspondence, and who

28

was therefore informed of the place of my residence. In this letter my brother expressed a great anxiety that I should join him at Ithaca, in New York, where he was then working in a morrocco factory connected with a large tannery. He had already made arrangements with the owner of the tannery that I should have work in the same tannery in the currying shop. Being equally anxious to be with my brother, I bid farewell to Johnstown, where I had enjoyed very good treatment, and went by railroad, then leading by a number of inclined planes across the Allegheny Mountains to Hollidaysburg, at the foot of the other side of the mountain, and from there by stage to Bellefonte, Williamsport, Elmira, then called Newtown, to Ithaca, where I was gladly welcomed by my brother, Henry.

Ithaca

According to previous arrangements I immediately entered upon work in the currier shop, and found my new situation in the society of a brother very agreeable. My employer and family, Mr. Robert Pelton, was of a very agreeable disposition and the village of Ithaca, at the head of Cayuga Lake, a very pleasant place to live in. I remained at Ithaca about ten months, when brother, Henry, in the spring proposed that I should go to the Blockhouse in Tioga County and see whether there would be an opening for a tannery in that section, as we learned that a large German settlement was made in that country .

Blockhouse

In compliance with this proposition I left Ithaca by stage to Painted Post, where I had a chance with a returning coal sled to ride up the Tioga Valley to Covington, and from Covington with the landlord, William Hagenbuch, in a sleigh to the Blockhouse Inn in Liberty, Tioga County. One principal reason why we had selected the Blockhouse as the possible place of our settlement in business was the fact that an old friend and customer of our father had established himself there as a farmer and I therefore first went to his house, and was hospitably received as the son of an old friend.

It was but natural that all the Germans of the neighborhood should be anxious that my brother and I should

29

commence a tannery in the place, and I was so much more inclined to meet their wishes as I had formed intimate acquaintance with the daughter of Leonard Schanbacher my father's friend, with whom I was then staying, which acquaintance finally ripened into marriage.

I bought a piece of land, 16 acres, to which I soon afterwards added thirty-three or more, near the Blockhouse where, after being joined by my brother, Henry, we erected a small tannery and on the same piece of land was a large log house, built by a German doctor and preacher, who had abandoned it, which house was occupied by us as a dwelling at the time, when we commenced in business. The township of Liberty was in good part very wild and the farms but small clearings in the woods with log houses occupied by the farmers as dwellings.

A large part of the population was German and Pennsylvania German, with a sprinkling of English and Irish people. They were mostly poor, having either expended all their capital in the purchase of their lands or never having had any means to pay for the lands, living on land purchased by contract at long credit of landholders, who were mostly very lenient in the extension of such credit. Some of the landowners, as the Bingham estate, would take grain or cattle in payment for land which was a great help to the early settlers, as money was very scarce and hard to get in those times. This scarcity of money was very detrimental to our business, as we could not obtain money for our leather, and therefore, had to sell it on long credit. These circumstances discouraged my brother, Henry, so much that he, being still unmarried, left me again six months after we had commenced our business, leaving me to struggle on alone.

Our small tannery being not well secured for winter and not being able to carry on my business on account of the severity of the winter weather, I accepted the position of teacher of one of the first common schools established, and taught both German and English for three months in the Schanbacher school district. I met with much difficulty in introducing discipline among the pu-

30

pils, who had grown up, without having ever seen the inside of a schoolhouse and had therefore to encounter many contests with pupils and refractory parents.

During this first winter my oldest son, Henry, was born, and the responsibilities of a father added. After the close of the school I resumed my business of tanning and farming on a very small scale. Times were very hard during the years 1837-38-39, the harvests of these years being very poor and the price of grain and bread-stuff very high. During these hard years we were flooded with shin-plasters, issued by companies and individuals, and the financial system was in a deplorable condition, bank failures being an almost daily occurrence. During these times my life was a continual struggle to provide means to make a living. I taught school a second winter and improved my small farm somewhat.

In the fall of 1840 the great presidential contest was fought and the people, anxious for a change, were fully roused to change the administration which had been democratic for several terms and William H. Harrison, the Whig Candidate for the presidency, was triumphantly elected. At this election I cast my first vote, having been just before naturalized, with the Whig Party with whom I remained as a worker, struggling with the minority in the county of Tioga, until the organization of the Republican Party in the year 1856.

Naturalized. 1840

Merchantile Business

In the fall of 1840 several Germans residing in Liberty and having confidence in my integrity and honesty, offered me a small capital to commence a store in Liberty, which offer I accepted. Mr. Updegraff, one of the most influential merchants of Williamsport and afterwards president of the West Branch Bank, and subsequently of the First National Bank of Williamsport, kindly furnished me with letters of recommendation to wholesale merchants in Philadelphia. With my small borrowed capital of $1,500 and these letters of recommendation my credit in the city was so good, that I was able to select a very good stock, of goods and I committed the error, common to inexperienced business men to purchase too much stock, for which I could find no ready sale, and which, therefore, remained on my hands too long.

While everybody expected a sudden change for the better after the change of the administration, times grew worse—a reaction having taken place in the finances of the country. Many had gone into speculation wildly, while everybody could make his own money during the life of shin-plasters. Money became so scarce that the state was obliged to issue what was then called Relief notes, which took the place of the irredeemable shinplasters. The bankrupt act was passed and many had to go into bankruptcy, and in consequence of the failure of Boyd and others whom I had trusted with the produce taken in payment of goods, I suffered very heavy losses which were soon increased by the failure of the Towanda Bank, the notes of which constituted most all Our currency. All these circumstances combined to bring me into a very embarrassed position and hindered me to pay my city debts contracted as well as to make payment of. the borrowed capital, but I continued to struggle on until every cent of my indebtedness was honestly paid, although it required many years of hard struggling, till I was again a free man. I remember with gratitude the many favors and leniency of my creditors, who never lost faith in my integrity, but patiently waited until I was enabled to discharge my liabilities. The best years of my life were in this struggle passed and were years of sorrow and full of trouble.

My brother, Henry, had established himself in Scalp Level, seven miles from Johnstown, Cambria County where he commenced a small tannery and had married, but soon after, in the summer of 1840, had lost his wife by death. I visited him after the death of his wife, traveling all the way from Liberty to Johnstown partly on foot and partly by stage. He afterward married again and raised a large family. He continued the business of tanning on a small scale, was also engaged in the mercantile business, but, like myself, never succeeded very well in business.

On the Fourth of July, 1840, we had an addition to our family by the birth of a second son, Gustavus, and in 1842 and 1843 by two daughters, Louise, and Mary. In the year 1845 I was elected justice of the peace, which office I held for three terms (15 years) and which was a source of more annoyance than profit.

In 1856 I was elected as County Auditor, which office I filled for three terms (9 years). This office brought me more to the notice of the Republicans of Tioga County, who, since the year 1856 had full sway as a party in the county, and in the year 1866 I was nominated and elected Associate Judge of Tioga County for a term of five years.

When the War of the Rebellion of the South commenced, in the year 1861, after the election of Abraham Lincoln by the Republican Party, both my sons were grown up to manhood and I deemed it right and proper that at least one of them should enter the service in defense of the nation and my adopted country, and Henry, the oldest, enlisted in the Co. D, 106th Regiment, Pennsylvania Volunteers, and soon after left for the seat of war along the Potomac. During the following winter, when the army was in winter quarters, he was sent home as a recruiting officer and in the vicinity of Liberty and Wellsboro was successful to enlist many recruits, whom he escorted in several squads to the recruiting headquarters at Harrisburg.

Henry's Death

When the army, under General McClellan, moved to the Peninsula all the soldiers and officers received orders to join their respective regiments and Henry, in May 1862, joined his regiment at Yorktown, went through the battle before Richmond, but when the army arrived at Harrison Landing he was taken with chronic diahorrea and finally paralysis of the limbs and yielded his life on the 14th day of August, 1862, as a sacrifice for his country. As the army was then moving toward Washington it was impossible to send his body home for burial, and he was buried at Harrison Landing, and after the war removed to City Point cemetery, where his remains now rest.

With us many other families mourned the death of sons, fathers, husbands and brothers, who fell in defense of their country and the Union. In the year 1863 our

33

second son, Gustavus, also left our home in the emergency, when the rebel hordes had invaded Pennsylvania and threatened Harrisburg and Philadelphia, and served in the 28th Regiment, Pennsylvania Militia on the borders of Maryland, but at the battle of Gettysburg the rebel army was defeated and retreated again passing the Potomac into Maryland and Virginia and Gustavus, after a service of about six weeks was discharged and returned home. He was soon after married and with myself carried on the tanning at Liberty.

Mary's Marriage

Our daughter Mary soon after was married to William Irvin, the brother of our son's wife, who then went into partnership with Gustavus in mercantile business and tanning. In the year 1866 they erected a new building for a store attached to the tannery. This proved a very poor speculation as goods depreciated in value very much and dissatisfaction arising, the partnership existing between Irvin Bros. and Veil and Son was dissolved, and William Irvin, our son-in-law moved to Canton, Bradford County, where he and Mr. Gleason built a steam tannery which they afterwards much improved and enlarged, doing an extensive and profitable business.

After having served as Associate Judge a full term (5 years), I was again elected County Auditor for a term of three years, which term, by the adoption of the new constitution, was lessened one year, so that I served but two years. Only a short time afterwards, in the spring of 1875, I received an offer of the position of, Commissioner's Clerk, which offer I accepted, as hard

Wellsboro

work in the tannery did not very well agree with my health. I purchased a home at Wellsboro, and after having resided in the township of Liberty for thirty-nine years I removed in May, 1875, with family consisting of my wife and oldest daughter, Louise, to the county seat, Wellsboro, and entered into the duties of the office of Commissioner's Clerk.

While this office was very laborious, it suited me well and I filled the same until April 1878, when, by the sudden death of Thomas B. Bryden, who had been elected Treasurer of Tioga County, the office was made vacant

34

and the Commissioners had to fill the same by appointment of a Treasurer. While there were over thirty applicants for the position it became very difficult to make a selection, and the choice finally fell upon me and I was appointed Treasurer of the County for the unexpired term, two years and nine months, almost a full term, while Mr. Leonard Harrison was appointed Commissioners Clerk to fill the vacancy occasioned by my appointment. After having given my bonds required, I entered immediately upon the duties of my new office. It was but natural that my appointment was the cause of much envy and ill feeling on part of disappointed applicants, but as I had not in any way solicited the appointment, my conscience did certainly not accuse me of having done any wrong in accepting the appointment, which gave me a more easy berth than the office of Commissioner's Clerk, while it, at the same time, brought better remuneration, although much more responsible. While I am writing these lines I am still holding the office of Treasurer, as my term will only expire at the first day of January, 1881.

Brothers' and Sisters' Families

While I have given the history of my own life up to the present it will be well to refer to a brief retrospective outline of the history of the other members of our family. My oldest sister, Dorothy, was as above alluded to, married in the year 1821 to Ludwig Kraiss. They raised a large family, especially boys, of whom seven emigrated to America.

(1) Henry, the oldest of the sons arrived in 1845 and lived with me for several years; He now resides in Union Township, Tioga County, on a farm and has raised a family of four sons.

(2) Charles carried on harness making for a number of years in Liberty, and then removed to Canton, Bradford County, where he accumulated much property and raised a family of three sons and one daughter .

(3) August, who came to America with Charles and Gottlieb, died single at the house of his brother Charles at Liberty.

(4) Gottlieb was a tanner and lived with me a num-

35

ber of years, afterwards carried on a tannery several years in the village of Liberty, sold the tannery to Albert, a younger brother, and moved to Jackson, Lycoming County, where he had purchased a farm, on which he now resides with a family of six children.

(5) Ferdinand, a harness maker, worked some time with his brother Charles at Liberty and at Towanda, established himself at Tioga, where he did very good business with his trade as harness maker, accumulated considerable property but was carried away by a kind of religious fantacism, being a member of the Jerusalem Friends, a sect which believed it the duty of the people of God to set up the kingdom of God and to erect at least a spiritual temple at Palestine, the Holy Land. These people being mostly Germans, had organized themselves as a colony and settled at Haifa, at the foot of Mt. Lebanon (Carmel) and at an inlet of the Mediterranean Sea. Ferdinand and his family joined them and is now living at Haifa, where he had to undergo great hardships and much sickness in the family.

(6) Paul, a cabinet maker, also located at Tioga, where he now resides, prospering in business.

(7) Albert, who bought the tannery at Liberty of his brother Gottlieb, carried on the tanning business some time, then sold the tannery and is now engaged on a farm near the village of Liberty, which he had purchased before he sold the tannery.

Three of my sister Dorothy's children remained in Germany and are still living there in the homestead of their deceased parents at Schorndorf.

My brother Henry died in March, 1877, aged 75 years, leaving a large family of three sons and five daughters.

The oldest son, Charles, entered as volunteer, during or at the beginning of the great War of the Rebellion, in the U.S. service, was promoted as orderly of General Ord, and served as such under several of the Corps Commanders, and at the battle of Gettysburg he rescued the body of General Reynolds, whose orderly he then was, after he fell pierced by the balls of the attacking rebels, and brought him within the Union lines. He accompanied the escort of the remains of General Reynolds to Lancaster, where the sisters of the General thanked Charles personally for the rescue of their lamented brother's body from the hands of the rebels. They donated to him the General's gold watch and many other keepsakes and promised their assistance for his promotion, if he would enter the regular service. He then enlisted in the First U. S. Cavalry and soon after received his commission as Second Lieutenant, was afterwards promoted as First Lieutenant and went with his regiment, the First U. S. Cavalry to Arizona, where he remained several years, and after being brevetted Major was discharged when the regular army was reduced.

He then went with a brother officer into the business of milling in Arizona, having built a steam grist mill for that purpose. They had extensive contracts with the U. S. government for the supply of flour to the Indian agencies of the Indian Territory. After doing a very successful business he sold his shares to his partners and came East and purchased at Canton the Canton steam mills, remained a few years at Canton but did not succeed very well. In the meantime his partner in Arizona failed to make his payments and Charles became embarrassed and was obliged to resume the ownership of the mill in Arizona with all the incumbrances resting upon it. He left his brother Henry in the management of the Canton mills, but as he could not make the payments yet due on the Canton Mills, they were sold and he lost all he had paid on the same. Besides this loss he left a heavy burden resting upon Charles Krise, who had signed with him for large sums of money. After the sale of the Canton mills his brother Henry left again for Johnstown where he and his brother John are in possession of my brother Henry's tannery.

My brother Gottlieb remained in Schorndorf in possession of our old home, engaged in tanning and in the cultivation of lands attached to it. He had several daughters but no son and died eight years ago—suddenly on his way home from a visit to our youngest brother, Chris-

37

tian, at Heidenheim. He died at the depot at Gmund, fifteen miles from home, his youngest daughter being with him.

Our youngest brother, Christian, who had chosen a mercantile career, having served his apprenticeship at Kirchheim, served as Comis. at Stuttgart, Frankfort, and Rheims and Metz mostly as bookkeeper, on his return to Schorndorf married a widow Schaal, went into business as merchant at Schorndorf. After the death of his first wife, which occurred a few years after his marriage he was re-married and moved to Heidenheim where he established a large woolen factory, but died suddenly three years ago, leaving the oldest son in possession of the business, the younger son being now employed at Ulm as professor of languages.

Caroline, our second sister, was married to Louis Illg, a baker at Stuttgart, where they continued in business and raised a family of sons and daughters. After her husband's death, Caroline, with the assistance of her oldest son, continued their business for several years, when Caroline died, six years ago, leaving as my only sister surviving with me, Louise, our youngest sister, who was married to Gottlieb Stumpf, also a baker of Stuttgart, who has always been very successful in business, and according to reports has accumulated much property in Stuttgart. They are still living but I have not heard from them for some time.

Of the seven brothers and sisters only myself and sister Louise remain on this side of the river of death, all the others—Dorothy, Henry, Gottlieb, Caroline, and Christian have passed over and on the other shore await bur coming to be reunited with our parents who have gone before. Mother, in the year 1848, and father, in the year 1850. What a solemn thought—a reunion with those beloved ones, from whom I had been so long separated by the intervening ocean, and how much should this prospect of a blessed immortality quicken us, to use all our time and means of grace to reach the haven of Eternal Rest, where the sails of our barks, after the many storms of life, may be furled.

38

As in this autobiography and the recital of incidents of my life I have not referred to my religious experiences or inner life of the soul, I deem it in place here to insert my religious or spiritual history. As above stated in giving the history of my youth I was educated in the Lutheran Church, being the state church of Wurtemburg and after having received the usual catechistic instruction for two successive years I was confirmed in 1827, with the class of 1813. I had very serious impressions during these instructions, but as they were not followed up by proper ministerial guidance the religious impressions were of short duration.

During my stay at Stuttgart, I attended church regularly on Sunday mornings and on my return to Schorndorf, I found that my sister Caroline and brother Gottlieb had associated themselves with the Moravians, called Pietists, and were attending their prayer meetings. They invited me often to accompany them to these meetings, but I had little faith in the character of these people, and no doubt judged them with prejudice, although many of them while great professors of divine grace, did not adorn their profession with a godly walk and conversation. One of the leaders of these Moravians, or Pietists, Jacob Veil, had a son Frederick Veil, who was my steadfast friend, and by his exemplary conduct and Christian character prompted me always to respect the Christian religion. I lived a moral life and shunned all the vices so common among the youth, and had the fear of the Lord in my heart which prompted me at the dark hour, when I seemed to be almost forsaken, to thank God on my knees for His deliverance. This took place at Bishofsheim, when I had been without work for a long time, and therefore reduced to the utmost destitution and distress of mind, as will appear by reference to the history of my journeys in Germany. But at the same time I was destitute of a saving knowledge of Christ, nor was the spirit of God witnessing to my Spirit that I was a child of God. My religious character was mainly built upon education and an innate veneration of God. When I settled in married life in Liberty I found a class of people there

39

mostly Germans, who made a profession of having been born again by the Spirit or being converted. They held many public meetings which I attended and at which I was struck with the emotional expressions and the physical symptoms of what they called the workings of the Holy Spirit, such as leaping, jumping, clapping of hands, failing to the ground, without sign of life, shouting, and many other outbursts of emotion. As I found upon examination of the characters of these people manifested in common life, that they were well meaning and deeply interested in the working out of the soul's salvation and in general no deceivers or hypocrites. I was bewildered and unable to account for these demonstrations.

Having a great confidence in the religious experience of the friend of my youth, Frederick Veil, I asked an explanation of him in a long letter in which I sought to give : him a full and unprejudiced account of all these demonstrations with an outline of the doctrines preached by their ministers—called Evangelical preachers—who then visited the Blockhouse periodically, every two weeks, preaching in private houses and in barns, to large congregations assembled from far and near. In these early times many would consider it no hardship to walk from four to eight miles after their day's work was done, to attend preaching or prayer meeting and return home the same night. In due time I received an answer to my inquiries of my cousin, Frederick Veil. He wrote a full and long letter in which he stated that since I had left Germany he had traveled extensively, that in his travels he came to England where he remained some time. While in England he got acquainted with Methodists, among whom he observed the same emotional symptoms at their religious meetings as described by me and upon the nature and cause of which I had sought information of him. My cousin stated that from his intercourse with the Methodists in England he learned that they were generally very sincere and earnest Christians, although many of them often were carried away by emotional feelings.

In fact my cousin seemed to have formed the same estimate of the character of the Methodists in England as I had myself observed here in America among the people calling themselves members of the Evangelical Association, a church founded at the beginning of this 19th Century and sometimes known by the name of German Methodists or Albrights. Their church doctrines and government being almost identical with the Methodist Episcopal Church in America.

Regarding those outbursts of emotion during religious exercises which puzzled me so much and which seemed in my way, my cousin advised me in his letter not to be deterred by them from seeking for an evidence of my acceptance into the favor of God by faith in the merits of the Savior Jesus Christ, but at once to accept the easy terms of the Gospel and to seek the pardon of my sins in the blood of Christ.

He gave me in his letter the explanation of these symptoms, as it had been given him by some enlightened Methodists in England. He illustrated the position and feelings of a sinner convicted of his sins, by comparing it with a convicted criminal upon whom the sentence of death had been passed and who was led to the scaffold, where the sentence of the law was to be executed. When the terror of his ignominious death was fully upon him he cast his eye over the multitude surrounding the place of execution, and away off in the far distance he sees the dim outline of a rider with a white flag, the symbol of pardon held aloft. Hope at once springs up in his anguished heart, and as the courier approaches, and the words "Pardon, Pardon" are carried to the ears of the convict joy overmasters him, and will manifest itself either by loud exclamations of joy, by leaping, clapping of hands, or even at times falling to the ground, with life seemingly suspended. So the sinner convicted by the law, and feeling the sentence of eternal death hanging over him at the faint glimpse by the eye of faith of his Savior, approaching with the cross-the emblem of pardon, by his merits removing the penalty of sin, will be similarly affected, and will manifest his joy in the same manner as the pardoned convict.

This illustration had the effect to remove many of the

41

obstacles in my way, to seek Jesus, although I never believed, nor do I now believe, that these emotional feelings are a sure index of the spiritual standing and state of the persons so affected.

My Own Experience

I attended the preaching of the Evangelical ministers more frequently and was fully impressed with the doctrine of conversion and regeneration of the heart, so earnestly urged by them. But having always led a moral life I was too prone to rely upon my own self-righteousness, and, therefore, could not perceive in my blindness the necessity of my own conversion. While I, at the same time often felt uneasy and concerned about my soul's salvation, I continued in this state for sometime, and notwithstanding the many warning and remonstrances of the members of the Lutheran Church, in which I had been elected as Elder, but which was in a very low state of religious spirituality (standing) I attended the preachings of Evangelical preachers whenever opportunity offered.

ESSICK
(Frank Sawyer: Liberty)

In the summer of the year 1837 I attended a Camp meeting held on the land of Christian Enig (?), in Liberty and when after preaching, those who felt themselves sinners and desired to receive pardon of their sins were invited to come forward to the so-called mourner's bench, to pray and to be prayed for, curiosity prompted me to come near to the altar to see and to hear. While I was quietly listening an old brother, who showed more zeal than knowledge, took hold of me to lead me to the mourner's bench, when old Adam fully awakened in me and I grew so angry that I tore myself loose from his grasp and went away, full of wrath and passion, to the outskirts of the Camp grounds, where the scoffers and enemies of the cause of Christ received me with exultation. But they had mistaken my character entirely. While I was angry at the act of the old brother their scoffings and profane language disgusted me to such a degree that I left them again immediately and returned to my seat in the congregation. While there the passion roused cooled off, upon an honest examination of my own heart.

Yielding

Disturbed by the last outburst of anger, I at once felt

42

my sinfulness, and the evil disposition of my heart, to such a degree that all my selfrighteousness vanished, and my eyes were fully opened to my true state as a sinner. While I was debating in my mind what to do, (my prejudices against an open and public seeking of the grace of God and pardon of my sins, being still very strong) my wife sent word to me that she was willing to go forward and seek religion and the pardon of her sins, if I would only join her. This message prompted me to throw all obstacles and prejudices to a side and surmounting all scruples I went forward and in the midst of a crowd of mourners I humbled myself and earnestly prayed for the pardon of my sins.

All the noise and tumult around me no longer embarrassed me and my anxious soul now burdened with a heavy burden of sin, earnestly cried to the Savior for pardon and acceptance. After a struggle of several hours I was enabled finally to grasp my Savior by faith, and peace which passeth all understanding entered into my yearning heart. I found the pearl of great price and unutterable joy filled my soul.

Conversion I do not know whether I praised God with a loud voice, or made any such demonstrations as I had observed in others who had passed from death unto life, but I do know that my soul was filled with the oil of gladness and that everything around me appeared as filled with the Glory of God. I shall never forget the time nor place, when and where I first found my sins forgiven, and when the evidence of my adoption first entered my heart, so that I could cry Abba Father.

Myself and wife both went home from that, to me, holy ground justified and rejoicing in the new born hope of eternal life, resolving to serve God, who had done so much for us, faithfully unto death. I am well aware that such a religious experience as I have given in my own case may be subject to the criticism of many who believe that there is no necessity of so much emotion and feeling, nor do I hold or believe that every conversion should necessarily be accompanied with excitement or sensation to be genuine. But one thing is certain—that a person

43

must feel that he is a sinner in the sight of God and His law, and must under that conviction of sin, be anxious to escape the penalty of sin. He must feel sick enough to inquire for the physician of the soul Jesus Christ before he can be healed from the malady of sin. He must by faith appropriate to himself the merits of a crucified Redeemer, who atoned for the sins of the world and feel the power of the blood of Christ applied as the healing balm of Gilead, to the cleansing and renewing of his own heart.

As to the degree of distress of conviction, or to the degree of the burden of sin resting upon the soul, the length of the struggle with the dominion of Satan, and with unbelief, the measure of joy entering the soul when the penitent by faith takes hold of his Redeemer, there certainly can be no rule laid down by which we must be governed. While every person may have a different religious experience, they will all unite and agree that they know that they have passed from darkness to light, from the dominion of Satan to God, and that God's Spirit witnesses to their spirit that they are children of God. After my conversion I separated from the Lutheran Church and was received as a member of the Evangelical Association which connection I continued to hold up to the present time.

Join Evangelical Church

In the beginning of my spiritual life I was very reserved and timid for some time and my voice was not heard in public prayer, while my conscience continually accused me on account of this neglect of my Christian duty. This reserve and cowardice, which kept me from an open confession of Christ, I finally overcame by the grace of God, and was soon after elected as class leader , which office I filled for many years. The duties connected with it were calculated to remove the fear of man, and I became more free in the exercise of my duties.

Local Preacher

In the year 1871, I was recommended by the quarterly Conference to the annual Conference at Baltimore for license as local preacher, which license was granted to me by said Conference. For several years, up to my removal from Liberty to Wellsboro, I attended to the duties

44

of local preacher, frequently filling the appointments of the absent preacher, sometimes for months, so that I got well acquainted with the several appointments of the circuit and meeting with much kindness on the part of the members of the congregations.

It was always a source of gratification and pleasure to be so engaged in the service of my Master, and I cheerfully devoted my time, and underwent the hardships of traveling from one appointment to another and proclaiming the glad tidings of the plan of salvation. As I attended during the time to my temporal affairs I had little leisure to prepare my sermons, but had to rely chiefly upon the assistance of the grace of God to declare the Word of God. However, imperfectly I may have done the work I have the satisfaction to know that my weak efforts were acceptable to the people, that at least some wandering souls were led to the feet of Jesus and to seek an interest in the blood of Christ, by my feeble efforts.

Removal to Wellsboro

On account of my removal to Wellsboro, where our church is not represented, and my time being fully taken up by my attendance upon the duties of the office, this active service in the cause of religion ceased. Although often importuned to join the M. E. Church here, I could not yet dissolve my ties with the Evangelical Church, whose servants and ministers had been instrumental in my conversion and in which I was born spiritually and raised although not united as a member with the M. E. Church. I have made my home with them, and attend the public and social services and worship at their church, but do not yet feel entirely at home. My long association with the Evangelical Church, its tenets and rules, and my extensive acquaintance with its ministers still rendering it my choice preference.

My views upon the subject of the doctrine of holiness and perfection, which agitated the minds of so many Christians, especially in the Methodist churches are so fully expressed in a letter written by me to Rev. Josiah Bowersox, now presiding elder in Oregon, that I can do no better than to insert it here, as my present belief upon that important subject.

45

Rev. Josiah Bowersox,

Dear Friend and Bro. in Christ:

Your welcome favor was received in due time, and I was glad to learn that you and family are in the enjoyment of good health and fully contented with your new situation.

Especially was I comforted to find you so kind in forgiving my negligence and remissness in my correspondence. It seems very difficult for me to get at letter writing no doubt on account of press of work I postpone to a more convenient time what should be done at once.

I was very much pleased with your exposition of the doctrine of sanctification and find that we agree nearer upon this subject than I was aware of.

When I disagreed with Bro. Rishel it was more about the mode of presenting the subject than about the doctrine itself. Bro. Davis of Milton, who preached a sermon here upon the subject of Sanctification, presented it like Bro. Rishel in an improper way, taking the position that gradual growth developed by the struggles with sin and the devil, as taught by himself before he obtained the great blessing of sanctification, was all wrong, arid by the exercise of sufficient faith and by a full consecration we could obtain that strength to overcome at once, and to become perfect.

It is certainly a lamentable fact too conspicuous not to be noticed by every discerning person, that there is entirely too much confidence placed by the generality of the members of the different branches of Methodism upon their experience of religion (which, of late, with many is very light and faint) and consequent adoption as children into the family of God.

This confidence in a once felt experience of the forgiving love of Christ often leads and lulls them into a sense of self complacency and security detrimental to progress and improvement in the well begun work. This security and consequential want of improvement and progress in Christian life, fully accounts for the many cases of back sliding and slackness in the performance of Christian duty, and the exercise of those Christian virtues which adorn the true Christian, and make him the light and the salt of the earth.

Many rely entirely upon their feelings, and their religion only based upon the sandy formations of feelings. They neither seek nor gain an increase in knowledge, grace and power so necessary and inseparable from true religion. If, to such Christians (?), the subject of sanctification and entire consecration to the Lord is presented in the mode in which I heard Bro. Rishel and Bro. Davis offer it to the people ,they may, prompted by their feelings, even experience the second blessing, so-called, and therefore, consider themselves fully sanctified, having, as they may, honestly believe, the evidence

46

of such Christian perfection or sanctification in their hearts and may really believe what they profess. This experience, founded upon feelings, is not calculated to remove that sense of self complacency and security spoken of above, so detrimental and antagonistic to progress in divine life.

While these views may not meet with your approval, I believe if you will, by the assistance of your experience as a minister, make a close observation of the lives of Christians generally, you will find at least some truth in my remarks and as you have given me full liberty to speak my views I will do so honestly, promising to yield to better arguments, for it is in the interchange of opinions upon these subjects that we obtain light and understanding.

I firmly believe, and the word of God plainly teaches, that it would be below the high privileges of a Christian to abide by the first principles of the Christian religion, but hold that it is his perogative, yea, his bounden duty, if he would continue in the enjoyment of the favor of God to go on to perfection. Martin Luther well remarks "Das Christenthum ist nicht ein Wesen sondern ein Werden es ist nicht geshehen, aber es ist im Gange und Gehwange." I hold that the sincere Christian is able by the grace of God and assisted by the virtue and Power of the blood of Christ, which cleanses from all sin, to overcome all evil, and, after repeated victories, to grow so strong in faith, based upon past experience and the promises of the word of God, to become of the full stature and manhood in Christ Jesus.

Yea, I go a little further than even you or those whom I have heard to preach upon the subject of holiness go. When you say that we may never expect to reach Ademic perfection while I believe with you that Adam was created morally pure and innocent, his fall at the first temptation offered by Satan, and his disobedience of an explicit and plain command of God, does not prove to me any superiority of position. If we could not aspire to as high. a position of holiness and perfection and the quality and quantity of our holiness should be less than that of our first parents, who fell at the first temptation, how could we ever claim perfection at all, with such an inherent proneness to fall. No, I believe that our experience of the many attacks of Satan, the enemy of souls, and of the many victories achieved by the help of the grace of God, makes us wiser and stronger to overcome temptation and the wiles of the devil, than Our first parents were, who had no such experience. Let us look to Christ, who ought to be our pattern, and in whose footsteps we ought to walk. He was also tempted by the same Satan with much more subtilty, but boldly withstood such temptations and defeated all the attacks of the enemy of mankind, and thereby

47

gave us an example how we ought to overcome the evil one.

While I believe in a continuing growth of divine life, I do not doubt that by a full consecration, founded upon self-knowledge and feeling of our dependence on God, and by fully relying upon the promises of God, by the exercise of faith, we can obtain a greater degree of grace and strength to overcome evil, proportionate and dependent upon our sincerity and earnestness to serve God and to love Him supremely with all our might, mind and strength.

But such an experience, desirable and precious, is but a bold step forward, in this progress of divine life and assimilation to divine nature and the image of God, lost by the fall of Adam and Eve and attainable by and through the atonement of Christ, may be restored within us.

I can conclude with no better wish and prayer, but that God may give us abundant grace to love Him supremely, and to consecrate ourselves to his service fully and unreservedly.

With my best wishes,

Yours,

C. F. Veil.

Such were my impressions upon this important doctrine of the Christian religion. Sanctification, years ago, and I have no reason to change my opinion upon the subject since I commenced this year with feelings of deep gratitude for God's preserving care. I have now almost reached my seventieth year, the age allotted to man, and, although feeling the common ailments of old age stealing upon me, I am comparatively still enjoying good health, with the exception of heart disease, which has been since several years as a thorn in my flesh. As walking seems to stir up the disease more than any other exertion, it deprives me of the privilege to attend public worship and social meetings as regularly as I had been in the habit to do formerly.

Being still able to be useful in many ways where exertion is not much needed and anxious to pass my time in useful employment, I have during last year taken up again the art of drawing, which I learned in my early youth, and succeeded so much above my expectation, that I made a number of ink drawings which now adorn our home, and are admired by all who feel an interest in such works of art. It is a cause of much satisfaction to me, that although far advanced fin years, my hands have not lost their cunning and steadiness, nor my eyes their clear sight, to enable me to do such intricate and fine work without the help of spectacles, for which blessing, in consideration of the state of my eyes in my childhood and youth, I feel duly grateful to God.

North Bend

During the last few months—November and December, 1882, I was with my son-in-law, William Irvin, who had built at or near the mouth of Young Woman's Creek at North Bend, Clinton County, Pa., a large tannery, which he was operating with about thirty hands or workmen. While there I was engaged to get the books in order, and to keep the books of running accounts, and as a store is connected with the tannery there was abundant work for me. While I was there I observed with sorrow the entire disregard of the Lord's Day, and with a hope to bring about a reform in that respect I proposed to hold public worship and preach on Sabbath which proposition was accepted. I was very much gratified to observe the good order and attention to the Word of God on the part of the congregation.

One of the landowners, who resides at North Bend, took the fancy to build a neat church with spire, in a fine grove near his residence, at his own expense (the basement of the church being intended for a school). This fancy on his part is so much more remarkable, as the builder is not a man of large means, nor does he make any profession of religion. At the same time there was a house for public worship now used by the M. E. congregation in the vicinity, amply sufficient to meet the wants of the people. After I had preached several times at this church, now used by the M. E. Church, Mr. Webster, the builder of the new church, who had heard me preach, made the proposition to me to hold services regularly every Sabbath at his new church, which I consented to do, as far as the state of my health will permit me.

Return to Wellsboro

I returned from North Bend to my home at Wellsboro on the 3rd day of January, 1883, and was accompanied by a grand son and grand daughter who intended to attend the Wellsboro graded school. I shall, if my health permits, return to North Bend after a stay or

49

vacation at home of about three weeks—as I have been urged to return as soon as possible.

After remaining a few weeks I returned to North Bend where I was expected to assist in the settlement of the store accounts, which I had found upon previous examination to be in such a bad condition, and showing a continuous loss in the store from commencement that William Irvin had insisted to close his connection with the store. Soon after my return an offer was made by a merchant of Renovo to rent the store at $400 per year, and to take all the remaining goods at cost prices, which offer was accepted by Gleason and Irvin and thereby removed all difficulties of settlement. As the store remained in the hands of the old firm until April 1, I had still the management of the store and tannery books and therefore remained until the new firm had taken possession of the store and all matters relative to the same had been satisfactorily arranged.

My health remained quite good during the winter and, in accordance with promise made to Mr. Webster, I held religious services every Sabbath in his church for some time, but I found very soon that the Methodists became suspicious that these meetings at the Webster Church would prove detrimental to their interest and concluded to keep aloof and to discontinue to attend the meetings. When I spoke to some of the leading members upon the subject, they freely confessed that the only reason for their absence from the meetings at the Webster Church was the fear of receiving injury to their organization and antipathy to the character of Mr. Webster. Relative to the last point, I had for some time had misgivings, and when about the same time, on account of some difficulty in the family of Mr. Webster, the regular meetings were interrupted by Mr. Webster himself, I was in one sense glad to have cause to discontinue the same, as I did not wish to cause any injury to the only religious organization then struggling for support in that vicinity.

About the middle of April I left North Bend and returned home and found them all well. Our grand children were still at school and quite at home at Wellsboro. After being at home about a month I received a telegram requesting me to come to Lock Haven to attend a suit pending between Gleason and Irvin and Bennett about the contract of delivery of bark to the tannery. I left home with Charles Irvin (the school at Wellsboro having closed) and went in his company to Lock Haven, Charley going on to North Bend. After remaining a whole week at Lock Haven, William Irvin and myself returned to North Bend where I remained until I had brought the books in order.

Conference at William

I omitted above to mention that during my previous stay at North Bend, in the beginning of March, 1883, I attended the annual session of the Central Pennsylvania Conference at Williamsport, where I had the great satisfaction to meet many of the old preachers with whom I had been acquainted and many of whom I had not seen for many years. At this Conference, on motion of some of my old friends, my ordination as deacon was granted, having been long previously in a probationary state as local minister, as I had no opportunity to attend a Conference and little anxiety or desire for ordination.

While in attendance at Conference I also met our son Gustavus, who was on his way to Reynoldsville, in Jefferson County, w here he intended to fill the position of assistant manager of a large tannery then being built. My son had lost his tannery by fire in the fall of 1882, and on account of the scarcity of bark in Liberty and vicinity had come to the conclusion to seek a new home and made arrangements to go to Reynoldsville, where his family moved during April, 1883.

During the summer of 1883 I remained at home working in the lot, etc., and after gathering all the products from the garden myself and wife went, by the new Pine Creek road, which had been opened during the summer, on a visit to our children and other friends. We arrived safely on the same day, when we left Wellsboro, at North Bend and found our children and grand children quite well and glad to see us.

After a good rest at North Bend we started for Reynoldsville to visit our son's family. We found them also well, but our son was not very much pleased with his situation, as he had the oversight over the Leach and Liquor Department of the tannery, which, on account of bark dust, very disagreeable. At the same time he was required to be in constant attendance from 12 o'clock noon to 12 o'clock midnight.

Reynoldsville is situated on the low grade or Bennett branch Railroad, leading from Driftwood on the P. & E. Railroad to Red Bank, intersecting there with the Allegany Railroad leading to Pittsburgh. After remaining at Reynoldsville about a week we returned to North Bend, where we remained until the beginning of December, my time being fully occupied in getting the tannery books in order.

Williamsport On our return we spent about a week at Williamsport visiting our friends. On Sunday forenoon I preached at request of the pastor, J. C. Reese, in the Bennett St. Church (the evening before having preached at schoolhouse near John Winters) .

About the middle of December, 1883, we arrived at home, after a very pleasant trip and visit of about six weeks. We found Louisa, our daughter, and Mell Veil, her cousin, well, and everything in order .

About New Year's I commenced to draw a copy of our house and surroundings, it being finished, I sent the same by mail to my sister Louisa in Germany, believing that she would appreciate it. Soon after I was attacked with the most severe cold and cough which I ever suffered connected with fever and have felt the effects of the disease for more than two months. This severe cold increased my old complaint, the heart disease, so that I was confined to the house the greater part of this winter. Having been debarred on account of disability and severity of the weather from attendance at church for nearly three months, I passed the time in making pictures of our old home in Liberty, of which I made three copies for our children and self.

During this winter our son, Gustavus, has changed his place of residence, from Reynoldsville to Clearfield, where he now keeps a meat market, and seems more pleased with his situation than at Reynoldsville.

This winter of 1883 and 1884 has been very severe and long, but very good for business of lumbering, etc., as there was good and long continued sleighing.

During the spring and summer season of this year I again passed the greater part of my time in the cultivation of garden and lot, and had the pleasure of seeing my labor rewarded by good prospects of fruitfulness. The work in open air seems to be the most congenial to my health and I am less subject to the attacks of heart disease while so occupied.

In the latter part of July my wife and I started on a visit to our son and family in Clearfield, where he then resided. We went by the Pine Creek Railroad to Jersey Shore, crossed the river to the station on the P. & E. Railroad, and along the same to Lock Haven, where we met Charley Irvin at the depot. After a few minutes conversation, we left by Bald Eagle Railroad for Tyrone, at the end of the road, and intersection with the great Pennsylvania Railroad (from Milesburg passengers are taken by a branch road to .Bellefonte, three miles from Milesburg—and back again to Milesburg and the main line). We arrived at Tyrone at six o'clock, p.m., and had to wait for the Clearfield train about two hours. During that time I accidentally met Rev. Samuel Seibert, who with his wife, was on his return home from the Lewisburg district, where he was holding meetings as presiding Elder.

About eight o'clock, p.m., we left for Clearfield—41 miles from Tyrone, but as it was growing dark we could not see much of the country. We passed through Philipsburg and near Oceola and Houtzdale, the most prominent points on the Tyrone and Clearfield road. At these places there was an unusual attendance of people at the respective depots, indicating a large population of the towns. We arrived at Clearfield at 10:30 o'clock, p.m., and found Lib and the girls waiting for us at depot and Gust a short distance from them with a buggy to take us to their home. We were very glad to find them all well and seemingly contented with their present situation.

53

We found Clearfield a very pleasant place to live in. The appearance of the town is much better than I had expected. It is regularly laid out and can boast of better private residences than any other town of the same size and population. Clearfield is well supplied with water works and gas and a company is organizing to heat the buildings by steam and have introduced steam for heating purposes in a number of public and private buildings in the town. Clearfield's situated along the West Branch River. First Street, where the most substantial and beautiful private residences are located faces the river and paralleled with the same run Second, Third, or Railroad Street, Fourth, Fifth Streets, intersected by streets deriving their names from trees as Walnut, Pine, Locust, etc., with Exception of Market Street in center of town. The Court House, to which of late a large addition costing about $45,000 has been made, occupies corner of Market and Second Streets. The most of the business by stores and otherwise is done on Second and Market Streets. The Presbyterian Church of stone and the M. E. Church of brick both on Second Street are very good buildings and ornaments in the town (the M. E. Church was then being repaired and beautified). On the other side of the river a new town has been commenced—W. Clearfield—which has a very nice situation and promises well. we remained two weeks at Clearfield and were quite favorably impressed with the town and its inhabitants. Our son, G. A. Veil, has a meat market on Second Street, opposite the Court House, and seems to do quite well.

On our return by the Tyrone and Clearfield Railroad we had a chance to see the great Horse Shoe Bend which shows even greater engineering skill than the Horse Shoe Bend on the Pennsylvania Railroad between Altoona and the Summit. As we intended to pay a flying visit at North Bend also, we stopped off at Lock Haven, took dinner at the Irvin House, where Charley Irvin called in the afternoon to see us. He told us that he would go home with us to stay over Sunday. I went with him to the Commercial School in the afternoon where I became acquainted with

Mr.Christy, the principal of the school. In the afternoon, at 4 p.m., we left with Charley and arrived at 5:30 p.m., at North Bend, where we found William Irvin with wagon to take us to their house. We found them all well and very glad to see us. They had made considerable improvements about the place, and built a house which was almost finished, to be occupied by William Irvin and his family, as they had rented the boarding house to Samuel Irvin. There was also a school house erected on the premises which will be of great advantage to the people living about the tannery.

After spending about a week very agreeably we left for Williamsport, where we also spent a week among our many friends in the city, and at Mrs. Christina Winters in the country, being everywhere treated with the greatest of kindness. We finally returned home after an absence of about four weeks.

Two months after our return we were gratified with a visit of Mary and her husband who accompanied her, Ida amid two little girls, Nellie and Jenny I and the baby, Bennie. William Irvin remained only a few days while Mary and children prolonged their visit three weeks, during which time we enjoyed their company very much. At the close of their visit Charley Irvin came here from Lock Haven, where he had just passed a course at the Commercial College, and after a few days visit here he left with mother and the children.

As we approached winter and the air became more cool and chilly, the attacks of heart disease became more frequent, and from November 1st I was confined to the house, as the least exposure to cold brought on those severe spasms of heart disease and stoppage of circulation of the blood. Finally, near the close of 1885, I was attacked with pneumonia, which was very prevalent during the winter in the county, and was the cause of death of many, especially aged persons. This attack connected with the old complaint prostrated me so much that my life was very much in danger for a few days, and it was hardly expected that I would survive. By the blessing of God, remedies and medicine prescribed by the attending

55

physician and the excellent care which I had by my wife and daughter during my sickness, brought about a change for the better, after having been confined in bed almost ten days. I was able to sit up, and from that time on continued to gain strength; The winter of 1884-85 was very severe, the thermometer indicating many times from 10° to 20° below zero. Even this morning, the 17th day of March, 1885, it showed 20° below zero, which is uncommon for this time of year. I hope and earnestly wish that we may soon have warmer weather, to enable me to leave the house, and enjoy the air, which, no doubt, would benefit my health.

During this winter before I was prostrated with sickness I took up the enlargement of photo pictures, which I had never before tried. I succeeded much better than I anticipated although it will require more practice to be perfect.

During the summer of this year (1885) my wife was also prostrated with severe sickness lasting several weeks, but thanks be to God, she recovered.* The whole year was more or less a year of affliction and suffering for us. I was troubled with more frequent attacks of my chronic disease and with periodical weakness of my eyes, which often prevented me from reading and writing. It has continued to trouble me ever since, more or less, until today, the 22nd day of August 1887, it is with much difficulty that I am trying to continue this biography.

Died July10, 1907 at 91 yr.

Died Oct-31-1887

Note

This autobiography was originally privately published by my great grandmother, Jenny Lind Irvin Hayes. She was the granddaughter of Charles Veil, and she is the same Jenny who makes a brief appearance on page 55.

The original edition measured six by nine inches. It was printed on buff textured paper and bound in a heavy paper cover, folded into one signature and stapled. Copies were distributed to various family members, by Grandma Jenny and by her daughter Mary Jane Hayes Hicks. Grandma Mary gave me her copy, which had her own notes in blue ball-point ink.

Recognizing the power of the Internet to make thesewritings more widely available, I have prepared two electronic editions of the *Autobiography*: a portable document file and a text-only file. I hope these formats will meet everyone's needs.

James H. Edgar
220 Winne Road
Delmar, NY 12054-4228
jhedgar@aol.com

Notes on the Portable Document Edition

Although the text has been reset, the pagination from page 3 to 56 is unchanged. The map on page 58 was originally 9-by-12 inches and stapled in the center fold of the book. Grandma Mary's handwritten notes have been reproduced in blue.

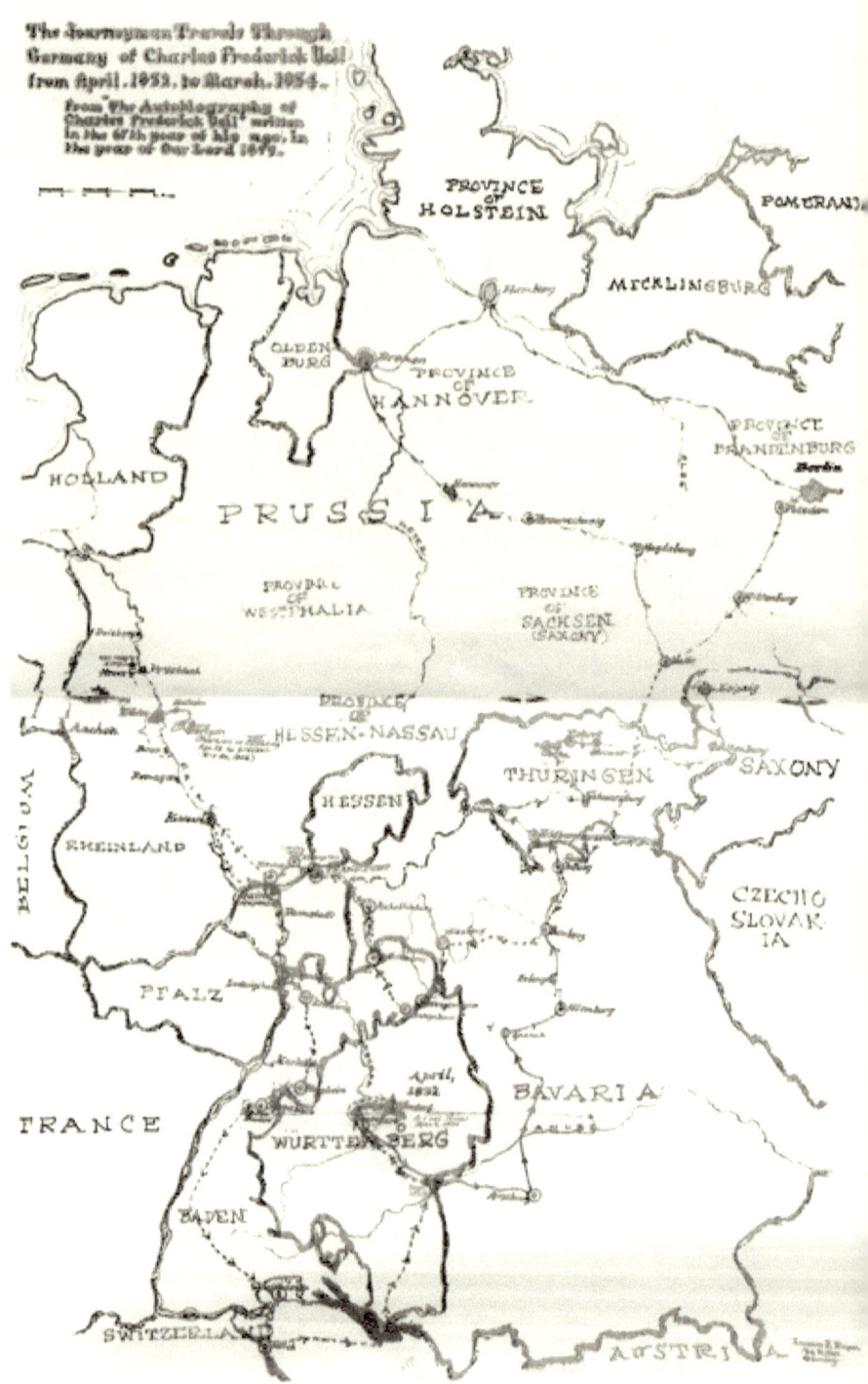

The Journeyman Travels Through
Germany of Charles Frederick Hall
from April, 1832, to March, 1834.

from "The Autobiography of
Charles Frederick Hall" written
in the 67th year of his age, in
the year of Our Lord 1879.

PROVINCE OF HOLSTEIN

POMERANIA

MECKLINBURG

OLDENBURG

PROVINCE OF HANNOVER

HOLLAND

PRUSSIA

PROVINCE OF BRANDENBURG

Berlin

PROVINCE OF WESTPHALIA

PROVINCE OF SACHSEN (SAXONY)

PROVINCE OF HESSEN-NASSAU

HESSEN

THÜRINGEN

SAXONY

BELGIUM

RHEINLAND

CZECHO SLOVAKIA

PFALZ

April, 1832

BAVARIA

FRANCE

WÜRTTEMBERG

BADEN

SWITZERLAND

AUSTRIA